Meri Paanch Kahaaniyan

Sharat Kohli

First Published in May 2020

ISBN: 978-93-90119-52-3

BLUEROSE PUBLISHERS

www.bluerosepublishers.com

info@bluerosepublishers.com

+91 8882 898 898

Cover Design:

Tyngshain Pariat

Typographic Design:

Ayushi Garg

Distributed by: BlueRose, Amazon, Flipkart, Shopclues

Preface

Story reciting and listening have been a tradition in our country since ancient times. May it be recited in any language, people of all age groups like to hear stories. Serials telecast on the television are one form of a story. The basic aim of my stories is to provide a message. My aim is to write these stories for youngsters and above. This is my first attempt to express my views in the form of stories. I sincerely hope that readers will like my work; else will enlighten me with better ideas for improvisation.

I dedicate this book to my late father who was always a source of inspiration to me.

Author Introduction

Completed schooling from Cambridge School, New Delhi, and graduation from Delhi University, I have over 28 years of work experience including working overseas as well. When working in India, had travelled overseas to organize international events. Writing and Dramatics have been my hobbies since my childhood.

Content

Chapter 1
Over Confidence or Misguidance

*****

Son of an army officer, Rohan had been good in studies, since childhood. So was he in the extra curricular activities. Studied in convent schools throughout, his mark sheets, report cards and the various trophies, won by him, proved him to be an outstanding student always.

Part of the few elite group of students who could gain admission in a prestigious institute, for professional studies, made his parents all the more happy and proud of him. On the basis of their son's performance, the parents were strongly of the view that their son can attain success in anything that he wants to do.

Rohan's paternal uncle, a government school principal, had a son named Mahesh. Studied throughout in government school and college, Mahesh was average in studies. On completion of the post graduation, Mahesh, along with his four childhood friends, started search for a job.

A friend, of Mahesh, named Suresh, got an opportunity to travel overseas, with family, and settle down their. After settling down overseas, the friend happened to meet a business person who was in need to get some ladies garments stitched. Suresh immediately advised this business person that the former could get them stitched from his country, to which the latter agreed.

Suresh immediately sent the details to Mahesh and the other friends; informing them that the order should reach him by the given date.

Mahesh and friends got on to the job and everything was executed on time.

A few weeks later, Mahesh and friends received a cheque, from Suresh, for the work they had done for the latter. Accompanied with the cheque was a letter, from Suresh, stating that this was the payment for the work they had done for the latter.

Over joyed by the receipt of payment, for the work done by them, Mahesh and friends decided to make this a full time profession.

The success ladder, when being climbed by Mahesh and his friends, was a source of inspiration for Rohan. Being bright and outstanding always, Rohan decided to settle down overseas; explore the possible business opportunities and get started with the one best suited for him.

Rohan expressed his views in front of his parents, who readily agreed.

On completing the required formalities, Rohan finally traveled overseas.

But as luck would have it, this was the turning point in the life of Rohan. He tried entering into business, but failed. He tried one line of business after the other, but success would not come his way.

Today, though he is settled abroad, but even after so many years, Rohan could not find success. He runs a small store which could never provide him the success that he may have attained, had luck favoured him. Though he married abroad but does not have a family.

On the other hand, Mahesh, after so many years, is an established garment exporter. He enjoys both name and fame; got married and the couple was blessed with a son.

Chapter 2
What To Say

*****

Simranjeet Rajagopalacharya and Rajadeep Dassmunshi completed their professional qualification, when in their mid twenties. Both found a good job, for themselves, in different private sector companies.

After settling down in their jobs, they decided to get married. Their parents agreed and the marriage ceremony performed. The newly wed couple, with the permission of Rajadeep's parents, decided to shift to the first floor of Rajadeep's parental house.

In less than one year of marriage, the couple was blessed with a new born baby boy. Everyone was happy. The new born was named Shradhanand.

All was well till the time Shradhanand had attained the age of 2 years.

One morning, while on the way to her office, Simranjeet, in her car, met with a road accident. She was seriously injured. Rajadeep was following Simranjeet, in his car, on way to his office. Rajadeep immediately jumped out of his car; rushed towards Simranjeet's car; took the latter out of her car; put her in his car and immediately rushed to a nearby hospital.

On arrival to the hospital, Simranjeet was declared "brought dead".

Shocked by the untimely loss, parents and relatives were plunged into sadness because of the irrepairable loss. Everyone grieving each other.

Mrs. Mansi Dasgupta, a senior IPS officer, was recently transferred here. She came and settled down in the next door house, owned by the Dasgupta's.

Shradhanand, while playing in the lawn, in the morning, would often see Mrs. Mansi Dasgupta going to her office, in the official conveyance. He would also see the latter in the evening, coming from her office, while playing in his lawn.

Mrs. Mansi Dasgupta would, in the morning, see Shradhanand playing in the lawn, with the grand parents taking care of him; in the evening would see Shradhanand playing in the lawn, with his father. Over the weekend, Mrs. Mansi Dasgupta would observe Shradhanand playing with his father.

One could often observe a smile on the face of Shradhanand while seeing Mrs. Mansi Dasgupta; while the latter felt a sense of pleasure in seeing the former.

One morning, on a weekend, when Rajadeep, accompanied with son Shradhanand, was driving the car out of his house; incidently Mrs. Mansi Dasgupta's car was also being driven out, by her driver, with the latter sitting inside the car. Both stepped out of their cars to officially introduce themselves to each other.

It was then that Mrs. Mansi Dasgupta came to know of Simranjeet Dassmunshi. Also, Rajadeep came to know of the former's husband, Mr. Om Prakash Dasgupta, who is a senior IFS officer and is posted abroad; and that they have 2 daughters who are married and well settled.

On serving the final 2 years of her career, Mrs. Mansi Dasgupta retired and settled down here. She now leads a retired life. Her husband, Mr. Om Prakash Dasgupta, would be retiring shortly and joining her.

Shradhanand is now 4 years old; goes to school; recognizes Mrs. Mansi Dasgupta well. The latter looks at the former as her grandson. Rajadeep has no plan of re - marriage as the memories of Simranjeet are fresh in his mind - and seem to remain so.

Chapter 3
Born To Die

*****

Ram Sukh and Kalyani were born to 2 different families, of Bijapur village, over 60 years ago. Both of them had working parents, who would work during the day and spend the evenings with their children. The children got good attention from their parents; were sent to the village school for studies.

After passing school, both Ram Sukh and Kalyani, found a job for themselves, in the village - with the help of their parents. Both were hard working.

When in the early 20's, the parents, of Ram Sukh and Kalyani, decided - it was time their children got married. Staying in the village for so many years, the parents knew each other and the children well. The parents met and the marriage was finalized.

After marriage, Ram Sukh and Kalyani shifted to a new house, which was close to the houses of their parents. They would go to work, together, in the morning and come back, together, in the evening. They would save a part of their salaries, so as to give good care and education to their would be child.

When, on the family way, the couple was very happy and would often dream of doing what all and what not for their child.

But as destiny would have it's way, the couple gave birth to a baby boy. The child was born with a medical problem. The couple made every possible effort, within their means, only to know that the child would have to live with the medical problem.

Kalyani had to leave her job so as to take care of their child [whom they had named Raja]; whereas Ram Sukh had to work over time so as to take care of the increased expenses and reduced income.

As Raja grew up, he showed interest in knowing more and more about new things. Kalyani would, as much as possible, explain them to Raja. She would also take out time to educate him in reading and writing.

As Raja grew up a little more, he started showing interest in poetry - trying to make and match new sentences and paragraphs.

Principal, of the village school, was informed about this. The Principal was surprised and happy; who started contributing his services by teaching Raja, free of cost.

At the age of 10 years, Raja compiled a small poem, which was checked, edited and completed by the school Principal.

This process began and by the time Raja attained the age of 14 years; he already had a few poems to his name.

Ram Sukh and Kalyani were really happy on this achievement; were also obliged to the school Principal. But major part of their heart was filled by the sorrow of the medical problem with which their son, Raja, was suffering. Also by the fact that they could not send Raja to school, which they had dreamt of.

By now, the medical problem, with which Raja was suffering, had started aggravating and becoming more painful. Raja, all this time, had faced this problem boldly; but now his courage had started to give up.

By the time Raja attained the age of 15 years, the medical problem had had a strong hold on Raja, which he could not face any more. He finally gave up and was gone, forever; only to remain in the memories of his parents and the residents of Bijapur village.

The poems compiled, by Raja, were given the shape of a book, by the school Principal. The book can be found in the school liabrary, which is very interestingly red by the students of the school.

Ram Sukh and Kalyani have now grown very old. Residents, of Bijapur village, take care of the old couple; never to let them feel alone or lost.

Chapter 4

Good Use of Habits is Good

*****

Deep, Sohna, Mandeep and Sohan have been childhood friends. They began their studies together, in the same class and school. Together, they successfully completed their post graduation.

While Deep joined her father, in his business; Mandeep got a job in a reputed multi national company. Sohna and Sohan passed a competitive examination and got selected for a public sector job, of choice.

Mandeep had the quality, in him, of imitating others, mono acting, etc. He would, at times, act as if he is hard of hearing, unable to hear complete words or sentences. His wordings and actions would be a source of entertainment for everyone hearing or watching him.

Deep and Mandeep also had an emotional attachment to each other. So did Sohna and Sohan. After settling down in their respective jobs, they got married.

After a year of marriage, Deep and Mandeep were blessed with a daughter [whom they named Rehana] while Sohna and Sohan with a son [whom they named Giriraj]. They took good care of their children.

The children grew up and were permitted, by their parents, to gain education of their choice. While Rehana gained education in Architecture, Giriraj in Software Engineering.

On completion of the post graduation, Giriraj got a job, through campus interviews, in a reputed multi national company. The company offered him a job overseas, which he readily accepted.

Giriraj informed this to his parents. Sohna was happy on Giriraj getting a job in a good company, she was sad on his overseas offer. Sohan satisfied himself by thinking that the overseas exposure would be helpful, to Giriraj, in further promoting his career.

Giriraj, finally, flew overseas and joined his job.

In the very first year, of the job, itself, he could impress the management with his knowledge and hard work. He got promoted, by the year end, accompanied with getting an official accommodation, of a senior level.

By the beginning of the second year, Giriraj had started getting emotionally involved with a colleague. Their attachment increased and they got married. Giriraj also decided to settle down overseas, permanently.

Giriraj informed his parents that he had got married and that he was, now, permanently settling overseas.

Stunned, the parents asked Giriraj - was he not required to inform them, of the marriage, in advance ? Also, how could he, on his own, decide of permanently settling down overseas? Do the parents have no right over him ? Have they done nothing for him ?

Nervous at so many questions coming his way, Giriraj replied – every parent does the best for their children. You have done so much for me; my career is taking an upward path. So what if I have found a life partner for me and have decided to permanently settle down overseas. You should be happy, for me, rather than putting so many questions at me. Sounding anoid, Giriraj disconnected the phone.

This was so much a shock for Sohna and Sohan, which they could hardly come out of, through out the rest of their lives. Trying to come out of this shock, Sohna and Sohan kept themselves busy, in their jobs. They retired on the due date and now lead a retired life.

Since the occurrence of this shocking incident, Deep and Mandeep have been regular in their visit to the house of Sohna and Sohan. Deep always expresses her concern in matters, small or big. With his imitating and acting qualities, Mandeep tries to keep the atmosphere happy. Rehana, like a daughter, shares her feelings with Sohna and Sohan as well.

Chapter 5
Competition Amongst The Intelligent

*****

Ram Sunder Dass and Shyam Sunder Dass are the twin sons of Dr. & Dr. [Mrs.] Ghanshyam Sunder Dass, both professors, in different subjects, in the State University. The sons, as their parents, are intellectuals but have interest in different subjects. While Ram has interest in animals, living or extinct, Shyam has interest in space studies. Both have always been interested in adding to their knowledge.

The parents, though happy for their children, would, at times, worry a little as they thought that the two brothers tend to compete with each other and this should not be a reason of rift amongst the two brothers. To take care of their worry, the parents decided that their sons write on their respective subjects. When completed, the parents would get the written material checked, from a group of 3 professors each, on both the subjects. This will help their sons to understand that they are both good in their respective subjects and have no reason to compete with each other.

Following is a part of the written material of the two brothers.

WRITTEN MATERIAL OF RAM

For millions of years, all life lived in the sea. It was home to a huge variety of creatures, such as shell fish, worms, sponges and jelly fish. None of them had back bones. About 510 million years ago, new kinds of animals appeared in the sea. They were the first fish and the first animals with backbones. Because they had backbones to support their bodies, they could become much larger.

The very first fish did not have jaws. It was called the jawless fish. It used to suck food into it's mouth.

The early fish were like giant sharks, much larger than any alive today, swam through the oceans. They hunted smaller fish. Armoured fish grew bony plates to protect their soft bodies. Other fish had bodies covered in sharp spines.

In the Indian Ocean is a fish called a coelacanth. It has hardly changed for 350 million years. It is a living fossil.

Some fish began to live in shallow water where it was difficult to swim. To help these fish move around, they grew short legs. Some of them also grew lungs, which meant that they could breathe air. These animals could live in water and on land. The lung fish is one of today's fish that can live out of water. It can breathe air.

About 400 million years ago, the first land animals – worms, spiders, scorpions and insects – evolved as they moved on to the land.

An animal that can live in water and on land is called an amphibian. It means "double life". The first amphibians appeared 350 million years ago. Gradually, they spent more and more time on land. About 300 million years ago, some amphibians changed into reptiles. They could live on land all the time. Reptiles have backbones and scaly skin, and most lay eggs. The first reptiles, such as Hylonomus, were small lizard like animals that ate tiny creatures. Reptiles learned to run quickly, so they could catch fast moving insects. As reptiles became larger, they caught and ate bigger prey. Some reptiles only ate plants.

Some early reptiles, e.g. Dimetrodon, had sails on their backs. It soaked up the Sun's heat and controlled the animal's body temperature. Some prehistoric reptiles grew fur on their bodies to keep themselves warm. These were the cynodonts. They lived about 245 million years ago. Over time they changed into a completely new group of animals, called the mammals.

Modern day crocodiles and alligators belong to the same reptile group, known as archosaurs, that the dinosaurs belonged to. This means they both have the same ancestors, which date back more than 230 million years. Dinosaur means "terrible lizards". They first appeared about 225 million years ago. For 160 million years, dinosaurs ruled the Earth. They walked on straight legs, tucked underneath their bodies and lived on land. Dinosaurs died out 65 million years ago. Many people believe this was because a big meteorite hit the Earth. It sent dust into the air which blotted out the Sun. Dinosaurs died because they were too cold and hungry.

At the same time as dinosaurs walked on the land, other reptiles flew in the sky and swam in the sea. The sky reptiles were pterosaurs, which means "winged lizards". Their wings were made from the stretched skin. Quetzalcoatius was an enormous pterosaur. It had wings 12 meters across. It is the biggest ever flying creature.

The sea was the home to various reptiles. Some had very long necks. These were plesiosaurs, which means "near lizards". Others looked like today's dolphins. They were ichthyosaurs, which means "fish lizards", and were fast and agile swimmers.

Mammals have backbones, their bodies are covered in hair or bristles, they make their own body heat and feed their young ones on milk. They have brains which are larger than most other animals. Mammals came to live in all of Earth's habitats. Many lived on land, but some, such as bats, were able to glide through the air on wings of skin. Other mammals, such as whales, dolphins and seals, swam in the sea. The first mammals appeared on Earth about 220 million years ago. They lived at the same time as the dinosaurs. Mammals survived after dinosaurs died out and became the ruling animals on Earth. There are about 4200 different kinds of mammals alive today.

Indricotherium was the largest land mammal. It was almost 8 metres tall and as heavy as four elephants.

Woolly mammoths were big elephants with extra long tusks up to 3 metres long. Their bodies were covered in fur.

Birds evolved from small, meat eating dinosaurs. Fossils show that some of these dinosaurs had feathers. They are called "dinobirds". The first dinobirds probably could not fly. Birds are animals with backbones, they lay eggs, can make their own body heat and have wings. They are also the only animals with feathers. Not all birds can fly. The first birds lived at the same time as the dinosaurs. The first true bird - a bird that could fly - appeared about 150 million years ago. It is known as Archaeopteryx, which means "ancient wing". It had claws on its wings.

The extinct bird Aepyornis laid the biggest eggs of all times. Each one was about the size of 150 hen's eggs.

WRITTEN MATERIAL OF SHYAM

Solar means "of the Sun". The solar system is centered around the Sun, the shining ball in the sky. It includes the family of nine planets orbiting the Sun, as well as the moons of these planets and the smaller objects such as comets, asteroids and bits of space rock. The powerful pull of an invisible force, called gravity, from the Sun stops these bodies from flying off into the deepest space.

The Sun is a star - a gigantic ball of burning gas. It has been shining for five billion years. Scientists estimate that the temperature at the Sun's core is around 15,600,000 degrees centigrade [28,000,000 degrees farenheit]. The pressure there is around 250 billion times that of the sea level on Earth.

The most extensive group of sunspots ever recorded was in the Sun's southern hemisphere, on April 08, 1947. It's area was about 18 billion square kilometers [7 billion square miles], with an extreme longitude of 3,00,000 kilometers [1,87,000 miles] and an extreme latitude of 1,45,000 kilometers [90,000 miles].

"Prominences" are large, eruptive features of relatively cool plasma, or iodized gas, at around 80,000 degrees centigrade [1,44,000 degrees farenheit]. Trapped within the Sun's magnetic field lines, they often form loops and can appear to twist and evolve above the Sun's photosphere for longer than a month. The largest to date have been around 5,00,000 - 7,00,000 kilometers [3,10,000 - 4,35,000 miles] long.

MERCURY is at a distance of 58 million kilometers from the Sun. It has a diameter of 4,878 kilometers. It has no moon. About one third the size of Earth, it would take 21 Plutos to balance one Mercury. The surface of Mercury is 350 degrees centigrade during the day and -170 degrees centigrade at night. It is the fastest planet. Being closest to the Sun, Mercury zooms around the Sun in just 88 days at an incredible 1,73,000 kilometers per hour.

VENUS is at a distance of 108 million kilometers from the Sun. It has a diameter of 12,104 kilometers. It has no moon. It is even hotter, as compared to Mercury, because it has clouds to keep in the heat. The mass of Venus is about four fifth that of the Earth. Venus spins on it's axis very slowly but orbits the Sun more quickly than Earth. A day, of Venus, lasts 243 Earth days but a year is only 225 Earth days. Named after a Goddess, Venus was the name of the Roman Goddess of love and beauty - just right for the planet, which many people think is the most beautiful object in the sky. Venus is sometimes called "the evening star".

EARTH is at a distance of 150 million kilometers from the Sun. It has a diameter of 12,756 kilometers. It has one moon. Earth is 4.6 billion years old. Nothing, at all, lived on the Earth for the first 1.1 billion years. It was a dangerous place where life could not survive. Life, on Earth, began 3.5 billion years ago. The first life appeared in the sea when it was hit by lightening.

MARS is at a distance of 228 million kilometers from the Sun. It has two moons. It has a diameter of 6,796 kilometers. Mars was named after the Roman God of war because of it's blood red colour.

JUPITER is at a distance of 778 million kilometers from the Sun. It has a diameter of 1,42,984 kilometers. It has seventeen moons. Jupiter is so big that other planets could fit inside it. At the center of Jupiter is a small rocky core, about as big as the Earth. Violent winds whip up storms all over Jupiter, but the Great Red Spot is the largest. Two Earths could fit inside the Great Red Spot, which is about 40,000 kilometers across. It has been raging away for almost 300 years. Jupiter's moon, Ganymede, is the largest moon in the solar system. At 5,276 kilometers across, it is bigger than Mercury.

SATURN is at a distance of 1,427 million kilometers from the Sun. It has a diameter of 1,29,660 kilometers. It has at least eighteen moons. It is the second largest planet in the solar system. It's rings are 2,70,000 kilometers across, about twice the width of the planet. It's moon, Titan, is the second largest moon in the solar system. Saturn is light enough to float.

URANUS is at a distance of 2,870 million kilometers from the Sun. It has a diameter of 51,118 kilometers. It has at least seventeen moons. Uranus is tilted on the sides. The poles, of Uranus, are the warmest places on the planet. They are even warmer than the Equator. Summer, at the south pole, lasts 42 years. Uranus was named after the Greek God of the sky.

NEPTUNE is at a distance of 4,497 million kilometers from the Sun. It has a diameter of 49,532 kilometers.

It has eight moons. Triton being the biggest at 2,706 kilometers across. Astronomers knew the existence of Neptune even before they could see it. Winds, faster than any winds on Earth, rip across the planet all the time. Triton, one of Neptune's moons, is one of the coldest places ever recorded. The temperature, in the ice covered moon, is minus 236 degrees centigrade. That's just 37 degrees centigrade away from being the lowest possible temperature in the entire universe.

PLUTO is at a distance of 5,900 million kilometers from the Sun. It has a diameter of 2,360 kilometers. It has one moon. It is the smallest planet in the solar system. Pluto was the name of the Greek God of the underworld. Also, the first two letter of Pluto, P and L, are the initials of Percival Lowell, who first predicted a planet beyond Neptune. Being the farthest from the Sun, Pluto is the coldest planet of all. Pluto's icy surface is minus 220 degrees centigrade. Pluto takes 248 years to orbit the Sun just once. For 20 years of it's orbit, Pluto dips in closer to the Sun, than Neptune. When this happens, Neptune is the farthest planet in the solar system.

A day is the amount of time a planet takes to spin on it's axis whereas a year is the time it takes to travel around the Sun.

Most people agree that the Universe began between 12 and 15 billion years ago. It all started with an explosion called the Big Bang. The Big Bang was super hot having a temperature of ten lakh crore crore crore [10 raised to the power 27] degrees centigrade. The effects of the blast were so strong that the Universe is still expanding.

The Big Bang could not happen in our Universe again. Some people think it may be happening millions of times, making millions of different Universes. Only a few would last as long as ours - most would pop like soap bubbles.

Some cosmologists [people who study the Universe] believe that the Universe will eventually stop expanding outwards. They think it will shrink back to nothing in an event called the Big Crunch. Even if the Universe does stop expanding, it will take about another 15 billion years to collapse in on itself in a Big Crunch.

On the other hand, some cosmologists think that the Universe will never stop expanding. They don't think gravity will ever be able to stop it, so it will just get bigger and bigger.

New stars are born in star nurseries - huge clouds of gas and dust known as nebulae [or nebula if you're talking about one]. The gases in a nebula gradually gather together into spinning balls. They spin more and more quickly until they get amazingly hot and a big blast, called a nuclear reaction, begins. When this happens, a baby star begins to glow.

The convection zone transfers hot gases to the surface of the star. The conduction zone carries energy from the core outwards.

The Sun is all alone, but some stars, called binary stars, are in pairs. They seem to spin around each other.

White giants are really huge, hot stars that appear to be white. They can be 20 times bigger than our Sun. Rigel is a white giant shining about 60,000 times more brightly than our Sun.

Really massive stars, at least eight times bigger than our Sun, die in an explosion called a Supernova. For a few days, Supernovas shine so strongly that, here on Earth, we can see them during the day. Supernovas are a very rare sight. Only a few have been seen in our galaxy in the last 1000 years. One visible to the naked eye was seen in 1987, in a nearby galaxy called the Large Magellanic Cloud.

A white dwarf is a dying star. It's gas has burnt off and a planet sized, white hot and incredibly dense core is all that is left. Over billions of years, this fades and dies. Sirius B, or the Pup, is a white dwarf. Once a white dwarf has cooled and stopped shining, it becomes a dead black dwarf.

A red giant is an old star that has swollen up. Depending on how big it gets, it might blow up or fade out. Astronomers think that our Sun will grow into a red giant in about five billion years time. Betelgeuse is a red giant and is 500 times bigger than our Sun. A red giant swallows up a planet.

Neutron stars are super heavy. They can be just 20 kilometers across but weigh 50 times more than the Earth.

Dark matter is what scientists call all the stuff, in the Universe, that they know is there but can't find. They think it might be made of ghostly little particles called neutrinos.

To make a trip to Proxima Centauri, our nearest star neighbour, would take 100 times more energy than our civilization currently generates. At 4.24 light years away, this red dwarf is the nearest star to the Sun. Even travelling at the fastest spacecraft speed achieved yet [Helios 2 at 252792 kilometers per hour {1,57,077 miles per hour}], it would take some 18,000 years to reach there. 2,68,136 astronomical units [4.24 light years].

1 astronomical unit is the distance between Earth and the Sun is roughly 149,597,870.7 kilometers [92,955,807 miles].

The distance between the stars is vast and is measured using a unit called "light years". One light year is the distance travelled by light in one year. The speed of light is 299,792,458 miles per second [671 million miles per hour]. One light year is the same as 9,460,730,472,580.8 kilometers [5,878,625,373,183.608 miles].

Our Sun is 8.3 light minutes away from the Earth and the Moon just 1.3 light seconds away

Near the center of the milky way orbiting this red dwarf star is OGLE - 2005 - BLG - 390Lb, the most distant extrasolar planet discovered to date. Even if we could travel at 252,792 kilometers per hour [157,077 miles per hour], it would take us 92 million years to get there.1.3 x 10 to the power 9 astronomical units [21,500 light years].

Gliese 581d, which lies in the "habitable zone" of it's solar system, is a contender for life. The "habitable zone" is the region around a star in which planets can sustain liquid surface water. A radio signal sent there in 2008 is due to arrive in 2029. 1.28 million astronomical units [20.3 light years].

TrES - 2b, around 750 light years away, in the constellation of Draco, reflects less than 1% of the light, making it darker than coal. The Jupiter sized planet has an estimated temperature of 1,200 degrees centigrade [2,192 degrees farenhiet], giving it a reddish glow. This darkness may be due to materials such as gaseous sodium in it's atmosphere.

Light moves most quickly in a vacuum, reaching 299,792,458 miles per second [983,571,056 feet per second].

A small number of galaxies are approaching our own M86, a tenticular galaxy around 52 million light years away, in the Virgo Cluster, is moving towards our milky way at 419 kilometers per second [260 miles per second].

A star, named SDSS J090745.O+24507, was discovered to be travelling at more than 2.4 million kilometers per hour [1.5 million miles per hour]. The speed was probably accelerated by an encounter with a super massive black hole at the center of our milky way galaxy near 80 million years ago.

"El Gordo" is the nick name of a massive galaxy cluster some 7 billion light years away. They are actually two galaxy clusters that are colliding at a rate of several million kilometers per hour. It's combined mass is around 2 x 10 to the power 15 times the mass of our Sun.

VFTS 102 is a star approximately 25 times more massive, than the Sun, and 1,00,000 times more luminous. It lies within the Tarantula Nebula in the Large Magenllanic Cloud, around 1,60,000 light years away. It rotates at an estimated 300 times faster than our Sun, at around 2 million kilometers per hour [1.2 million miles per hour]. If it rotated any faster, it would be in the danger of tearing itself apart with centrifugal forces.

Sagittarius A* is the super massive black hole that resides in the center of our milky way galaxy, some 27,000 light years away. With a mass around 4 million times greater than our Sun, this black hole is orbited by several massive stars.

NGC 4889, a super massive black hole, discovered in the center of the elliptical galaxy, is some 336 million light years away. It's mass is estimated at around 21 billion times that of the Sun.

Gamma ray bursts, the birth cries of black holes, are the largest explosions in the universe. At 2:12 EDT on March 19, 2008, a gamma ray burst in a galaxy, 7.5 billion light years away, was visible for 30 seconds and captured by a robotic telescope.

The latest observations of LBV 1806 - 20, which is 45,000 light years from the Earth, indicate that it is between 5 and 40 million times more luminous than the Sun. It has a mass at least 150 times the mass of the Sun and is at least 200 times the Sun's diameter.

Less than 0.1% of the stars, in our galaxy, are blue super giants. With masses of around 100 times that of the Sun, they burn through their fuel very quickly and can last as little as 10 million years. Their blue colour is a result of their high temperatures, around 20,000 to 50,000 degrees centigrade [36,000 to 90,000 degrees farenhiet]. One of the best known is Rigel in the constellation of Orion. It is the sixth brightest star in the sky, despite being around 900 light years away.

A huge wall, of galaxies, has been discovered which is some 1.37 billion light years long.

A dwarf galaxy is orbiting a large elliptical galaxy, 10 billion light years away.

Scientists have successfully imaged a galaxy so old that it's light has taken 13.2 billion years to reach us. This means the galaxy, as we see it today, was formed less than 480 million years ago after the Big Bang, making it the earliest object to form in the universe.

RESULT

The written material of Ram and Shyam was checked, by the respective group of 3 professors each. It was found that both, Ram and Shyam, have abundant knowledge, in their respective subjects. They are both outstanding students; at par with each other in terms of knowledge. There is no reason why they should compete with each other.

www.ingramcontent.com/pod-product-compliance
Ingram Content Group UK Ltd.
Pitfield, Milton Keynes, MK11 3LW, UK
UKHW042001190726
13854UKWH00005B/2115